MELOWY

The Song of the Moon

Danielle Star

Scholastic Inc.

Published by Scholastic Inc., *Publishers since 1920*, 557 Broadway, New York, NY 10012. SCHOLASTIC and associated logos are trademarks and/or registered trademarks of Scholastic Inc.

ISBN 978-1-338-15176-3

Text by Danielle Star
Original title *Il canto della luna*

Editorial cooperation by Lucia Vaccarino
Illustrations by Emilio Urbano (layout),
Nicoletta Baldari (clean up), and Patrizia Zangrilli (color)
Graphics by Danielle Stern

Special thanks to Tiffany Colón
Translated by Chris Turner
Interior design by Baily Crawford

10 9 8 7 6 5 4 3 2 1   18 19 20 21 22

Printed in the U.S.A.   40
First printing 2018

Contents

Imagine a magical land wrapped in golden light. A planet in a distant galaxy beyond the known stars. This enchanted place is known as Aura, and it is very special. For Aura is home to the pegasus, a winged horse with a colorful mane and coat.

The pegasuses of Aura come from four ancient island realms that lie within Aura's enchanted oceans: the Winter Realm of Amethyst Island, the Spring Realm of Emerald Island, the Day Realm of Ruby Island, and the Night Realm of Sapphire Island.

A selected number from each realm are born with a symbol on their wings and a hidden magical power. These are the Melowies.

When their magic beckons them in a dream, all Melowies leave their island homes to answer the call. They must attend school at the Castle of Destiny, a legendary castle hidden in a sea of clouds, where they will learn all about their hidden powers. Destiny is a place where friendships are born, where Melowies find their courage, and where they discover the true magic inside themselves!

Map of Aura

The Winter Realm

Maya

Her realm: Spring
Her personality: shy and sweet
Her passion: cooking
Her gift: the Power of Heat

Cora

Her realm: Winter
Her personality: proud and sincere
Her passion: ice-skating
Her gift: the Power of Cold

Selena

Her realm: Night
Her personality: deep and sensitive
Her passion: music
Her gift: the Power of Darkness

1

A Surprise for the Melowies

The Castle of Destiny changed at the beginning of every school year. The castle's silent corridors, high ceilings, and steep spiral staircases filled with laughter and friendship. The castle turned into a place where promising young Melowies came to search for their own destinies.

"Hey, girls! The first week of school is finally over!" cried Electra. She ran out of the science lab like a cyclone of red curls. "When do we start lessons in the Art of Powers? I can't wait to learn how to use mine! In the Day Realm, Melowies make beams of light! I wouldn't even know where to start."

"Not yet," said Cora, throwing cold water on Electra's enthusiasm. "First we have to take our core lessons, which will be hard. I almost fell asleep in pegasus science today!"

"Me, too!" Electra said. "But that's because I was too excited to sleep last night! Just think! We survived our first week at the Castle of Destiny! We made it!" She found a gap in the crowded corridor and skipped away.

Cora shook her head. "No one behaves like that in the Winter Realm."

"Come on, Cora!" teased Cleo with a chuckle. "Do you always have to be Miss Icicles?"

Selena was so deep in her own thoughts that she passed right by her two friends.

Maya, though, was still dragging her hooves. "Is something wrong?" asked Cleo.

"It's true. We have made it," whispered the pink filly. "But what if I'm not up to it? They have already given us a mountain of homework to do. I still haven't finished the geology project, and now we've got two chapters of science to finish by tomorrow!"

Cleo just smiled. "Come on, Maya! You're doing just fine. Even Ms. Pangea said so when you answered that question about the Spring Realm!"

Maya blushed. "Well, that was easy! That's where I'm from! But you got a ten on the first literature assignment. I don't know how you did it."

"I think it's because I really like reading."

"And you were fantastic at the first aerobatics lesson."

"Oh, that's only because I have been secretly watching flying lessons since I was little!" Cleo said.

Cleo was the only Melowy who didn't know which of the four realms she came from. She grew up at the Castle of Destiny after the school principal found her on the front steps when she was just a baby. She'd

never been allowed to mix with the students who lived in the castle, until this year. The day of the entrance exam, she discovered that she was a Melowy as well. All at once, her dreams had come true. Best of all, she made four new friends, each from a different realm.

"Come on! Ms. Calliope is waiting for us in the auditorium," cried Cora, urging her slowpoke friends along. Maya and Cleo hurried after her.

"Yippee!" The girls heard a voice from a floor below them. Cora, Maya, and Cleo all leaned out over the spiral staircase to find a cyclone of red curls dashing down the handrail. Electra was riding it like a slide!

Cora shook her head. "Why does she always have to make a scene?" she said, walking down the stairs slowly. Cleo and Maya chuckled, and followed her.

Once they were outside, they all flew across the garden. They went past the waterfall, which glittered with a thousand shades of blue and green. They flew over the heads of chattering groups of students and waved hello to the gardener, who was whispering to his beloved flowers. Finally, they arrived.

The auditorium was a huge room with beautiful tall windows. There were dozens of seats arranged in a semicircle around a stage with a purple curtain made of heavy velvet. There was a place for Principal Gia and the other teachers to sit above all the other seats. The first-year students sat around the stage in front of a lively looking pegasus.

"Come in closer! Come in closer!" Ms. Calliope called to the students. They were all looking around at one another timidly. She hadn't raised her voice at all, but her words rang across the entire auditorium.

"Where is Selena?" Maya whispered to her roommates. Cleo looked around and saw her standing near the doorway by herself.

"I have an announcement," continued Ms. Calliope with a shake of her mane. "I have decided that all the first-year students will have to do a special kind of test this year. Believe me, girls, it is going to be something very special."

2
Friendly Competition

"A musical!" exclaimed Electra with a huge smile as they left the auditorium. "Did you hear that? A musical!"

"Yes, we heard," sighed Cora. "We were there, too, you know."

But Electra continued, too excited to let Cora bring her down. "And the story is so beautiful! Two rival princesses who put aside their differences to defend their realms! I really hope I get to play one of them!"

"I would be much happier with a smaller role," said Maya with a shrug. "I mean, my singing is not so bad, but my dancing isn't the best. And the whole school will be watching us!"

"Come on!" Cleo smiled. "We can practice for the audition together!"

"That sounds like a lot of fun!" said Maya with relief. "What about you, Cora? What do you think?"

"Us Melowies from the Winter Realm have excellent singing and dancing teachers. I am going to try out for one of the leading roles."

"Good luck!" snarled a strange voice. The voice belonged to a Melowy with long blue-and-purple hair, and green eyes with a mean glare. "My name is Eris, and you are going to have to go up against me for a leading role."

"Wow, you are really modest, aren't you?" teased Cleo. But Eris pretended not to hear and walked away with her nose in the air.

"My mother taught me not to pay any attention to Melowies with no manners," Cora said, giving her long mane a shake.

"We'll see about that, you big show-off!" Electra shouted in the direction of Eris. Everyone turned to stare at her.

"Electra!" Cora sighed.

Selena, who'd seen everything, came over and joined her friends. "Selena! Why didn't you come sit with us before?" asked Electra as the girls crossed the garden. "Aren't you excited about the musical?!"

"I don't like musicals," said Selena as they turned down the dormitory hallway.

"What?!" cried Electra. "But everyone likes musicals!"

"Not everyone," muttered Selena, looking annoyed. "I don't. I also don't really like the idea of performing in front of people. Especially not after the last time . . ."

When they got to their room in the Butterfly Tower, Selena grabbed her drumsticks off her bed and started playing her drum kit. She had long ago promised herself that she would never perform onstage again. She played her drums loud to help drown out the memory of the last time.

"Hey, Electra!" Cora snapped. "Why is your skirt on my bed? How many times do we have to talk about this?"

"I'm sorry. I must have left it there this morning by mistake," Electra responded.

"You have to try to be neater!"

"Says the Melowy who has filled the bathroom with thousands of different bottles. By the way, why on earth do you need a lotion for polar climates? The weather's lovely here!"

"My stuff is perfectly neat."

"Sure, but where are we supposed to put ours? There's no room left!"

"Here we go again," Selena mumbled. "If this musical has as much harmony as we have in our room, it's going to be a disaster!"

3
Peace and Quiet

At breakfast the next morning, Selena got
herself some cereal and a cup of milk, and
looked around the crowded cafeteria for a
place to sit. She found her roommates sitting
together, eating and chatting. She sat next to
them, closed her eyes, and took a deep
breath. Selena enjoyed starting her day
slowly and quietly. She liked to eat her
breakfast in silence, sometimes while gazing
out the window.

"Hey, sleepyhead!" cried Electra. She shook her mane, still wet after her shower, which splashed water everywhere.

"Hey, watch out!" shouted Cora, whose mane was perfect as usual.

"So much for peace and quiet," Selena whispered to herself. She gazed out the window, missing her quiet mornings back home more than ever.

"Selena," Cleo called, distracting her from her sad thought, "we are all going to get some lunch and eat in the garden after class. Do you want to join us?"

Selena thought about it for a minute, not sure how to answer. She was not used to spending time with Melowies her own age.

Maybe it was time to change that, since she would be living with these girls for the next four years. She did like them after all, and it sounded like it could be fun.

"Yes!" cried Electra. "You should come, too, Selena, and then we can all practice for the auditions together! I have been practicing my favorite part, which is when Princess Cassiopeia orders her soldiers to defend her realm!"

Selena suddenly changed her mind. Everyone kept talking about that silly musical. She had not even bothered to listen to the songs that Ms.

Calliope had given them to learn. If she had to be in the musical, she would join the choir and hide in the back row.

"No, thank you," Selena answered. "I still have a lot of algebra homework to finish. I want to be ready just in case there's a pop quiz."

"Is this because you don't like musicals?" asked Electra. "It is going to be so much fun! You love rock music, right? There is a cool scene where the princesses' armies battle the witch's ghostly legions,

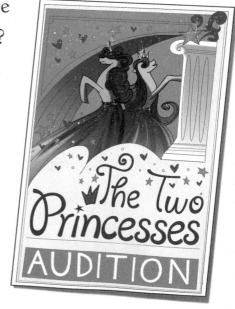

while the moon looks on and sings this really great song."

"No, really, I have homework," Selena repeated.

"Aww," Electra sighed, disappointed.

"Leave her alone," said Cora. "Algebra is a very important subject."

"And boring!" said Electra, making a face. "And impossible to understand!"

"Well, if you paid more attention in class, you might learn that you actually like it."

"Okay, you two, no need to argue," joked Cleo, standing up to fix her skirt. "Anyway, we should really get going or we will be late for our next class."

"Are you sure you don't want to come?" Maya whispered to Selena.

"I'm positive." Selena nodded.

The afternoon passed slowly for Selena, alone in her room working on her homework. She thought she could at least enjoy some peace and quiet, since the others were in the garden. But after a while, it was a little too quiet.

She looked down at her algebra book and snorted before throwing herself on her bed, feeling very gloomy. Just then, her cell phone lit up with a message from Electra. It was a link to a song. Selena rolled her eyes. Electra would not give up trying to persuade her to audition! She put on her headphones and pressed the play button. Suddenly, an awesome song came through her headphones. It was so good that she jumped up and started dancing. Music was Selena's favorite thing in the world. It could always make her feel better.

When the song ended, she dropped back onto her bed and picked up her phone. There was another message from Electra.

How cool is this song? It's from the musical. The next time we practice together, you have to come! You will love it!

"That song is from the musical?" Selena whispered to herself. It was one of the best songs she'd ever heard. Maybe she should give the musical a chance. If only she could find the courage.

4
A Twist to the Tale

The auditorium was crowded with nervous
first-year students when the day of auditions finally arrived. Cleo looked around.
She was surrounded by Melowies, each one
with a different story and each with a different symbol on her wings. Some of them
were daughters of doctors, teachers, and
warriors who had studied at the Castle of
Destiny before them. Others were the

children of pegasuses with no special powers and had made their parents so proud on the day they were chosen to come to the school. Others, like Selena, were the daughters of queens. Cleo thought it was such a pity Selena wouldn't be there to audition.

"Oh no! Oh no!" Maya kept repeating in between deep breaths. "What if I forget the steps? What if I fall flat on my face? What if . . . ?"

"Don't worry!" Cleo smiled. "I am nervous, too. But we've practiced a thousand times! You will be great."

Cleo and Maya had asked to audition together. They both wanted the roles of Princess Cassiopeia's ladies-in-waiting. Both were small parts, but they still had a big dance scene and the steps weren't easy.

"Who'd like to go first?" asked Ms. Calliope. Everyone in the auditorium went quiet and all the Melowies stared down at their hooves. All, except one.

"I do!" a confident voice called out from the crowd. It was Eris. She strutted up onto the stage, wearing a plaid skirt with rhinestones around the hem. Her long blue-and-purple hair hung loose over her shoulders.

"What a show-off!" whispered Electra, before Cora shushed her.

"What will you be singing for us, Eris?" asked the teacher.

"Princess Cassiopeia's aria, of course," snorted Eris. She closed her eyes and, with a theatrical gesture, began to sing. Her voice was beautiful.

"Well, I've got to admit, she can really sing," whispered Electra.

"Stop," Ms. Calliope suddenly cried.

Eris gave her an annoyed look. "But I haven't finished! There's still another verse to go!"

"I know," explained the teacher. "You have a very good voice, Eris, but that alone will not be enough. I want to see how you cope when the pressure's on. Electra, could you come up here, please?"

"Me?!" cried Electra in surprise. But she

did as she was told and took a spot on the stage next to Eris.

"Let's try it again as a duet, with each of you taking turns singing the verses," Ms. Calliope said.

"But it's a solo piece!" cried Eris.

Ms. Calliope only nodded and gave Electra the cue to begin singing. Eris immediately started singing even louder, trying to drown out Electra's voice. Electra just kept singing, doing her best, sounding more and more confident. Eris stared at Electra and grew angrier. She was so focused on winning that she forgot some of the words of the song and ran off backstage, embarrassed.

"You see, skill isn't enough. You need self-control, calmness, and awareness of others," said Ms. Calliope. She looked at Electra thoughtfully.

"I think you would be perfect for the role of Princess Cassiopeia," she said.

5
Now or Never

"Where is Selena?" asked Maya. The auditions had lasted three hours and were coming to a close. Everyone had done so well!

"She decided not to audition," said Cora. "She says she wants to be in the choir."

"Well, that's it, girls," announced Ms. Calliope. "I'd like to thank you all for your hard work and enthusiasm. There are still a few roles I haven't decided on, but we have our leading ladies, Princess Cassiopeia and

Princess Kalista, who will be played by . . ."
Again, the auditorium went dead quiet.
"Electra and Cora!" announced the teacher.

"*Yay!*" squealed Electra, rushing over to her friend to give her a big hug.

"Be cool!" Cora whispered, giving her a frosty look.

"Umm . . . congratulations, Cora," muttered Electra, giving her a timid pat on the back.

Ms. Calliope taped the list to the wall and let the excited Melowies see for themselves who had been given what role.

"We did it! We're the handmaidens!" cried Cleo and Maya in unison.

Eris had been given only a small role, but she did not know that yet. She was still hiding somewhere backstage, embarrassed about the way she'd ruined the duet. As the auditorium was emptying out, Ms. Calliope asked Cleo to try to find her.

"Me?" asked Cleo, feeling very puzzled.

"You're the one who knows her way around the school the best," explained Ms. Calliope.

"Please be quick, Cleo. We all want to go and celebrate with a milk shake at Sugar and Spice!" said Electra.

"You go and I'll catch up," said Cleo with a nod as she went backstage.

It was quiet except for the creaking of the floorboards under Cleo's hooves. And under someone else's hooves as well.

"Who's there?" called Cleo. "Eris, is that you?"

Suddenly, a familiar face popped out from behind a clothes rack full of costumes.

"Selena, what are you doing here?" Cleo said, startled.

"Well, umm, I don't really know." Selena stared down at her hooves.

"Did you change your mind about auditioning?"

"No. I—I—I mean . . . I don't know," Selena stuttered.

Cleo smiled. "There is nothing wrong with changing your mind, you know! I wasn't too excited about the musical at first, but now I love the idea. It has been really fun!"

"I didn't exactly change my mind. It's too late, anyway. The auditions are over."

"It's never too late!" Cleo insisted. "Why don't you ask Ms. Calliope if you can audition now? She is still here. But you will have to hurry!"

"You think I should?" asked Selena, looking up at her friend.

Cleo saw the excitement flash across Selena's face and nudged her toward the stage. Then she walked back to continue looking for Eris.

Selena found Ms. Calliope just as she was about to leave the room. It was now or never.

"Ms. Calliope," she called, unable to stop herself.

"Yes?" The teacher turned.

"I am Selena from the Night Realm. I asked to be a part of the choir. But I changed my mind. I would like to audition for the part of the moon."

"Why didn't you audition with the rest of the girls?"

"Well . . ." Selena blushed, but forced herself to be honest. "I didn't think that I wanted to be in the musical, or that I even liked musicals, until I heard the song that the moon sings."

"And you think that song is right for you?" the teacher asked, smiling. "Well, your name does mean moon. You are lucky: The role has not been filled yet. I have to point out, though, that role has an added difficulty. You will have to sing while flying around the stage wearing a very heavy costume. Do you think you can do that?"

"I would like to try."

Cleo hid behind a prop, watching Ms. Calliope help Selena into the moon costume backstage. She just had to see Selena's audition, but she didn't want to make her friend nervous.

"There. You would make a beautiful moon!" said the teacher, looking at Selena dressed in her costume of shimmering stars. "When you are ready, you may

begin." Ms. Calliope then sat in her seat in the front row.

Selena took a deep breath and started walking toward the stage. She stepped on her skirt and tore a big rip down the side! Cleo was about to run onto the stage to help her friend, but before she could move, Selena shook her head and a cascade of sparkles came from out of nowhere and fixed the costume up as good as new.

Selena had broken one of the most important rules at the Castle of Destiny! She used magic to fix the tear in her costume. And Cleo wasn't the only one who noticed. Another pair of eyes watched from behind the scenes. Now they shone with a wicked gleam.

6
Practice Makes Perfect

Selena took a happy trot along the maze of trails around the Castle of Destiny after the audition. She wanted to tell all her friends about the audition, but for now, she was just going to enjoy her moment. She felt wonderful, like singing onstage had taken a huge weight off her shoulders.

She stopped to breathe in the irresistible smell of vanilla, cinnamon, and berries in the air outside the Sugar and Spice café. She looked in the window to admire the beautiful muffins and pastries of every color and noticed her friends sitting at a table inside. When she walked in, the Melowies greeted her with a gloomy look.

"Is something the matter?" she asked them.

"I told everyone that you auditioned for the part of the moon," Cleo explained.

Selena shook her mane, suddenly feeling defensive. "Well, didn't you guys want me to be a part of the musical?"

"Of course we do!" Maya said. "It's just that . . ."

"I changed my mind, that's all. I decided it sounds like it could be fun. Why are you looking at me like that? Do you want me to say that you were right all along? You were right! I was wrong! I had fun auditioning. Are you happy now?"

Selena sighed and sat down with her friends. "Look, I have to tell you guys something," she said, blushing. "I really love music. That is why I nagged my mom until she would let me play the drums. But the first

time I ever played onstage a couple of years ago . . . well, it was a disaster! I sat down and saw my mom in the audience staring at me, and I just froze! I had nagged her to come see me, and then I got so nervous that I couldn't play. I got in trouble for wasting her time and money on the drum set."

"I am so sorry that happened to you!" Maya exclaimed. "That must have been hard. But you are older now. You will be fantastic, you'll see!"

"You will be the star of the whole musical!" Electra added. "Well, the moon, actually."

"Everyone gets nervous," said Cora. "But you can't let one bad experience keep you from trying again."

Cleo sighed. "I agree, but there's something we need to talk about."

"What?" asked Selena.

"You used magic," snapped Cora. "Cleo saw you. You know very well that using magic is against the rules!"

"Is that why you are all looking at me like that?" Selena laughed. "But it was nothing. In the Night Realm we do innocent little spells like that all the time!"

The other Melowies just stared at her with worried faces.

"Maybe in the Night Realm," said Electra, "but here at the Castle of Destiny, you are not allowed to. A real Melowy doesn't use magic like that. It's like . . . cheating."

Selena got up and walked toward the door. "Don't worry about me," she said. "I can take care of myself." She flew off, alone.

They practiced for the musical for the next couple of days. Little by little, Selena felt that she was losing all the confidence she had gained after the audition. Ms. Calliope was no help at all. She actually seemed to be much harder on her.

"It's not my fault!" Selena defended herself yet again. "Eris came in late!"

Eris raised her nose up at her. She was always trying to ruin everything Selena did,

and the Melowy from the Night Realm couldn't figure out why.

"It isn't about Eris," Ms. Calliope explained. "Selena, you are very good. But, for a musical to work, everyone has to pull their weight. You need to listen closely to what is going on around you and interpret your part. Please take a break and try again when you are more focused."

Selena went and sat on a bench with a gloomy expression. Maybe she had been wrong to audition for the musical after all. Maybe she wasn't right for the part and she would only embarrass herself again. Maybe she wasn't even that good and she didn't deserve to be in the musical.

When she looked up, she saw four pairs of eyes staring at her.

"Look, we know you can take care of yourself," said Cleo, "but that doesn't mean that you always have to do it on your own. We would love to help you practice."

Maya, Electra, and Cora all nodded in agreement. Selena looked at them for a moment and then nodded back.

7

Opening Night

"Wow, I don't believe it! The whole school is here," Electra said, peeking out from behind the closed curtain.

"Well, that was to be expected," said Cora.

"It's one thing to expect something and it's another to actually see it!" exclaimed Electra, still peering out at the audience.

It was opening night and Cora and Electra had to go onstage first to set up the story about the two rival princesses having to come together in order to defend their realms.

"You two look amazing!" Maya cried in excitement. Electra's costume was fiery red, while Cora's was emerald green. Their coats were covered in glitter, and their manes were

shiny and perfect. The two Melowies were ready to go onstage.

"Absolutely beautiful," agreed Cleo, still struggling to get into her handmaiden costume.

"Let me fix your sash," said Cora, seeing that Cleo was having some problems. She

gave her costume a skillful tug and a tuck and then smiled in satisfaction. "A perfect handmaiden. Your costume won't get in the way of your dancing now."

"What about Selena?" asked Electra.

"Here I am."

"Wow!" they all said in unison when they turned to look at her.

Selena's costume seemed to have been made especially for her. With a little bit of glitter, she looked just like a shining moon.

"Thank you, without you, I never could have done it." Selena blushed.

"That's what friends are for." Cleo smiled.

"Group hug?" squealed Electra.

"We would all get covered in glitter! Forget it!" Cora giggled.

"Of course, Miss Icicles." Electra laughed. "I wouldn't want to spoil your perfectly perfect perfection."

"Okay, girls, let's concentrate. The show is about to start," said Cora.

"Let's do our vocal warm-ups," Electra agreed.

"Wow," whispered Maya. "Those two are getting along!" Cleo and Selena smiled in response.

"Everyone come here!" Ms. Calliope cried, gathering all the Melowies around her to give them some last-minute advice. Then the young actresses took their places and the curtains went up.

Electra and Cora were great in the first scene. Cleo and Maya danced perfectly and were the funniest parts in the show. They made the whole audience laugh and clap.

"Now it is up to me," Selena told herself, pacing back and forth backstage. "I can do this. Everything is going to be fine."

Just then, an evil-sounding voice hissed, "So here she is, the wicked witch from the Night Realm." It was Eris. "I saw you, you know. You auditioned in secret, with no one watching so you wouldn't make a fool of yourself in public. As if that wasn't sneaky enough, you used magic!"

"You saw me?" Selena asked in shock. "But it was just a mistake. I didn't mean to . . ."

"Here you are with your big role, while I have been given a tiny, little part. Let's just see how well *you* do under pressure. I didn't tell on you just so I could enjoy this moment. Your scene is next. Better get going."

"Selena, onstage now!" called Ms. Calliope.

Selena took off with a flap of her wings. Just as she flew out onto the stage, Eris pulled on a rope off to the side. A moment later, something dropped right on top of Selena. She looked at her costume and saw that she was covered with green paint. She looked up and noticed the curtain had opened and the whole school was watching.

8
Applause and Hugs

The audience held its breath as Selena stood shocked in the middle of the stage. She couldn't let herself look silly performing again. She had to do something. Suddenly, silvery sparks shot out from her horn without her even wanting them to. This was just a minor setback, nothing a little magic couldn't fix.

"No!" she cried, suddenly coming to her senses. She shook her head and the sparks stopped. Back home, in the Night Realm, she could always solve her problems with magic. But she was at the Castle of Destiny now, and Melowies here did not use magic. They did not cheat.

Selena looked around. The Melowies in the audience were starting to whisper to one

another, confused and surprised by what was happening.

"My scene!" Selena whispered to herself. "I have to concentrate on my scene." So, with her costume completely ruined and her heart beating in her throat, she started to sing. This was her song. It was about her feelings. The moon was high in the sky, all by itself. But, just like Selena, it would have given anything to come down to be with the others. She let herself get carried away by the beautiful music. When the sound of her last note slowly faded away, the audience burst out in applause.

When the show ended, Ms. Calliope came to talk to Selena backstage.

"I am so sorry, Ms. Calliope," she pleaded. "I didn't think I should stop just because my costume was ruined."

"Selena, you were wonderful," the teacher interrupted her. "You were able to stay calm, and you were able to play your role despite all the difficulties. You were excellent!"

Selena felt her heart beating fast. Even the evil look Eris was giving her could not wipe the smile off her face.

"If you tell on me, I will tell everyone that you used magic during your audition," Eris hissed as soon as the teacher was gone.

"Thank you, Eris," Selena said calmly. "You did me a huge favor. Thanks to you, I learned that I can overcome anything without using my magic. Even when I can't do it alone, I have my friends to help me."

"We'll see about that!" threatened Eris, before walking off with a shake of her mane.

"Selena, you were fantastic! Incredible! Amazing!" cried Electra, running toward her.

"And incredibly brave!" added Maya.

"You should be very proud of yourself," Cora agreed.

"Come on! Let's take a curtain call!" said Cleo, nudging her friends back toward the stage.

"We were pretty good, weren't we?"

Electra said later in the dressing room, admiring herself in her costume one last time.

"Yes, we were, but you don't have to say it every five minutes," said Cora, who had already changed and showered.

"But she's right," said Cleo with a big grin. "If we don't hurry, we'll miss out on the party!"

Electra started taking off her costume but then suddenly stopped as the others were leaving. "Hang on! Group hug?"

she asked. Maya and Cleo jumped in first, dragging Cora with them. She tried to protest but didn't really seem to mean it.

Selena looked at them all, happy and covered in fiery red sparkles. "Here I come!" she cried, feeling happier than she ever had in her life.

Back in the Night Realm, the rain tapped against the castle window like frozen fingers. The four pegasuses paid no attention to the sound.

"We need someone inside the Castle of Destiny to help us," said one of them.

"A spy," agreed another.

The ruler nodded, making her crown of dark gems sparkle in the flickering candlelight. "There is one Melowy who's different from the others. A Melowy who might want the same things we want," she said with an evil smile. "Her name is Eris."

Read on for a sneak peek of the next exciting moment in the Melowies' journey:

The Night of Courage

A Strange New Teacher

The sun had been up for quite some time at the Castle of Destiny. The first-year students were already awake and in their classroom, waiting for their new teacher.

Suddenly, the door opened and a tornado swept in and swirled to the front of the classroom. Clouds of papers, pencils, and books flew up into the air behind it. The tornado settled into a Melowy wearing a leather jacket and cowboy hat that looked about a hundred years old. She also wore a few belts around her waist. The girls in the front row quickly realized that her breath wasn't as fresh as it could be.

It was *her*, every student's worst nightmare, the defense techniques teacher, Ms. Ariadne. The students whispered nervously to one another.

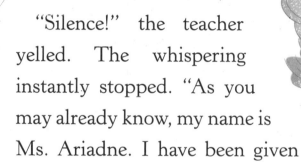

"Silence!" the teacher yelled. The whispering instantly stopped. "As you may already know, my name is Ms. Ariadne. I have been given the impossible task of teaching you weaklings how to defend yourselves. Let's not waste any time. Who can tell me why we study defense techniques?"

None of the Melowies dared to speak.

EXPLORE DESTINY WITH THE MELOWIES AS THEY DISCOVER THEIR MAGICAL POWERS!

Hidden somewhere beyond the highest clouds is the Castle of Destiny, a school for very special students. They're the Melowies, young pegasuses born with a symbol on their wings and a hidden magical power. And the time destined for them to meet has now arrived.

■SCHOLASTIC

scholastic.com

MELOW